Lucky James is ready to take
the animals to their new home.
But what are those naughty
monkeys up to?

Wait a minute.
What's that barking noise
coming from the shed?

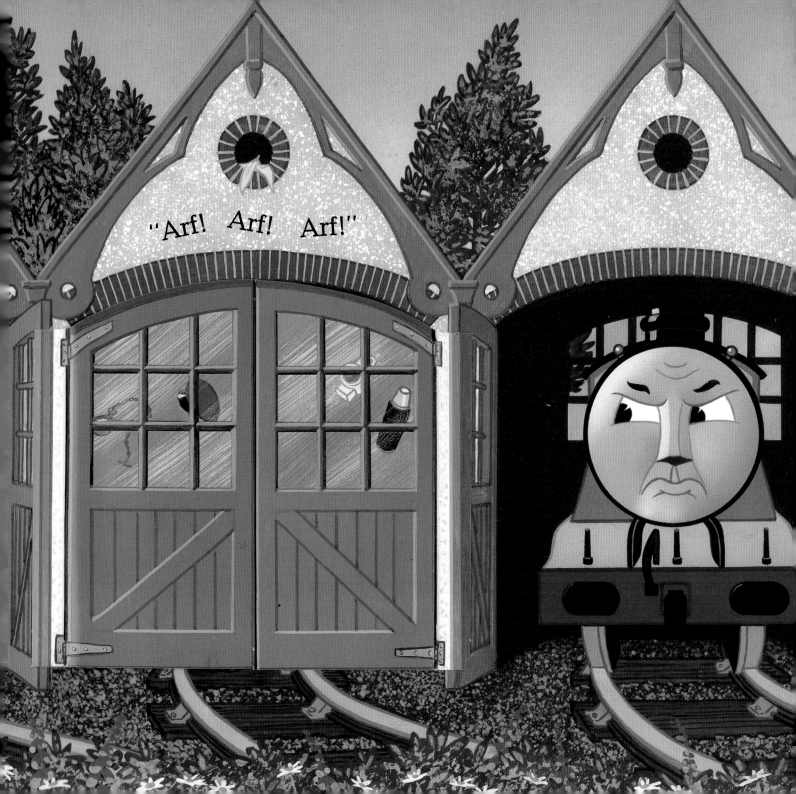

Who is shaking that bush?

And listen...
Let's look in the luggage car.

Oh no, Edward!
There's something fishy going
on in that freight car.

Sounds like a cat
in that shed.
What do you think?

Another delay?
No need to get in a flap,
Sir Topham!

We're almost ready to leave for the zoo.
Thomas must take on some water.

Thanks to Thomas and his friends,
all the animals have been rounded up.

And it's a good thing, too,
for it's almost...

...time for the Grand Opening of the zoo!